AF191500

SHOGUN DRACHENGOTT

YOU'RE THE SON OF A WHORE

RELIGION IS YOUR PRISON

novum pro

This book is also available as e-book.

© 2025 novum publishing gmbh
Rathausgasse 73, A-7311 Neckenmarkt
office@novum-publishing.co.uk

ISBN 978-3-99146-887-5
Cover photo:
Sakkmesterke I Dreamstime.com
Cover design, layout & typesetting:
novum publishing
Internal illustrations:
p. 20 © Imaengine I Dreamstime.com
p. 31 © Andrey Popov I Dreamstime.com
p. 32 © Tarragona I Dreamstime.com
p. 34 © Siloto I Dreamstime.com

www.novum-publishing.co.uk

Print product with financial
climate contribution
ClimatePartner.com/16547-2311-1001

"You son of a bitch!" "Your mother is a whore!"
"You're the son of a whore!"

What does it do to you when you read or even hear such sentences? Are you offended? Or do you not care? The most important is this statement: "You are the son of a whore!" That's exactly what I mean – because that's you! The same goes for if you're a woman. You're just the daughter of a whore. And – no! – I don't apologize for that. But I want to explain to you why I'm throwing something like this at your head:

You can't choose your parents, you might say. I'm going to disagree with you: you're just not aware of it. I also thought so earlier, until I gained additional knowledge. But, speculatively, even if it is true that you cannot choose your parents, you will agree with me that you have free will, even if you believe in fate and that everything is predetermined. In the case of fate, it is indeed the case that not everything is predetermined. Free will and some statements from the Bible have nourished in me the conviction that we choose our own parents even before we are born. Whether you can grasp that in the same way, I'll leave it in the room for now. I am convinced that we shape our own reality from birth.

Jesus was called the son of a carpenter. Similarly, "You are the son of a whore." Here it is the mother's background that makes me call you that. This book is about being able to choose your mother.

We are all just spiritual beings in one body. God "Jehovah" said: "Let us make man in our image." This statement in the plural indicates that several spirit beings, which can also be described as extraterrestrial, have come to Earth. In some scriptures, the Hebrew word elohim appears in the plural, as in this quoted statement from the Bible. It is important to understand how to understand the message that several Elohim have condensed their spiritual bodies into physical bodies. This raises the following question for Bible readers: Why, then, does the Bible tell us about only two people?

If the statement is to be considered in such a way that several creatures were simply involved in the human project, then the answer would be clear. But if several creatures became human beings, then the answer to why the focus is on only two people is that they have taken a certain action that has shaken the entire universe. I quickly realized that I am not a part of this world, or that I am not of this world, that has been confirmed. Man is an act of creation that can be traced back to beings of light, creatures who are often referred to as angels or gods. I also like to refer to them as spiritual beings. In the spiritual scriptures (such as the Bible, Qur'an, Tanakh and others) the source is also referred to as God or divine, and thus all people today have parents of origin.

By this I do not mean the biological parents, but our parents, whose origin we forgot in the incarnation. Isn't that interesting? You may be hearing or reading this for the first time.

Our parents of origin transfer our life into the physical body we have chosen, or we choose people who are ready to receive our soul: conception. The Incarnation is an act of the Spirit into the Incarnation. The sexual act is usually used for this purpose. In other words, we spiritual beings choose earthly human beings and use the sexual act to fertilize the egg cell as sperm. We spiritual beings are also able to transmit life directly. The birth of Jesus illustrates this: the angel Gabriel transferred the life of the Archangel Michael into Mary's womb. This is how we proceed, which is why I described at the beginning that we choose our parents. Whether you want to accept or reject this statement is up to you.

This book is about a certain mother, which is why I explain that you are the son of a whore. In the Bible, we learn that there is also the mother above (Jerusalem in heaven, Galatians 4:26, Hebrews 12:22). This book enlightens you on what is meant by the great whore of Babylon and why it is important to choose the right mother. And WHY you should leave your religion immediately.

The development of religion helps to understand what is meant by the great harlot Babylon (described in the 17th and 18th chapters of the Bible book of Revelation). Because we are spiritual beings, from the very beginning we have the need in our body to seek the divine. In doing so, we made use of religion. Even our ancestors – as primeval peoples still show today – used rituals and beliefs to make the supernatural comprehensible. Today's religion, however, has its origins in Babylon. Keeping this in mind helps to understand the verse-by-verse consideration of chapters 17 and 18 of Revelation!

BABYLON, THE GREAT WHORE

"And one of the seven angels who had seven bowls came and spoke to me, saying, 'Come, I will show you the judgment of the Great Harlot, who sits on many waters, with whom the kings of the earth committed fornication, while those who inhabit the earth were made drunk with the wine of her fornication.' And the Spirit of God carried me away into a wilderness. And I saw a woman sitting on a scarlet-colored wild beast, which was full of blasphemous names, and had seven heads and ten horns.

And the woman was clothed in purple and scarlet, and was adorned with gold and precious stones and pearls, and had in her hand a golden chalice full of abominable things, and she drank the blood of saints and the witnesses of Jesus. On her forehead was written, 'Babylon the Great Harlot, Mother of All Harlots.'" (Revelation 17:1-6)

A summary of chapter 17: The wild beast represents seven kings, five have fallen, one has already come, the other has not yet come. The Five Kings Who Fell describe five world powers from the past. The one, who has already come, stands for Rome at the time of writing. The other, who has not yet come, indicates the world power of the future – the Anglo-American world power. Since the kings represent world powers, the description of the harlot cannot be understood politically. The waters that you saw, where the harlot sits, signify peoples and multitudes, nations and their languages. Thus, the harlot exercises dominion over people. This becomes even clearer when it is explained that no musical instrument is heard in it. Weddings will still be solemnly held or customs will be celebrated. (Revelation 18)

In chapter 18, I want to focus on the fourth verse. There, the people are urged by Jesus himself: "Come out of her, my people." This call is clear and unambiguous. Take them seriously! Why should you take them seriously? Simply put, Babylon, the great harlot, is religion. Religion, along with politics, has exerted the greatest power over people – and that applies to any religion, even your denomination. As long as you are part of a religion, you are the son of a whore. Think about it. Do you want to be the son of a whore? Remember my questions at the beginning. If you don't mind, then you won't want to read on and you won't want to change. On the other hand, it should be important to you not to be a part of religion, as it will disappear.

The Catholic sect as well as the Reformed sect and other faith communities will be devastated by politics in the future, as it is symbolically described. If you struggle with it, you will disappear too. Only those who can put into practice the words of Jesus will experience true spirituality – the Mother above as well as the heavenly Jerusalem. For only those who become part of the greater whole and entrust themselves to God as the source of all spiritual things will live true faith.

Because when Jesus was on earth, he never wanted his ideas to become a religion. He wanted all people to be united in faith. Just as it is written that Abraham is the father of all believers. "Jehovah is the God of Abraham, Isaac, Ishmael, and not of the dead." So my spiritual father, the archangel Michael, spoke to Moses. At that time, you were dead, but alive in the eyes of God. Jesus had the great vision that people should learn that they are brothers and sisters, united in love and faith. It was never intended that there would be three rival religions. No Christians, Muslims, Jews – and no other religions, by the way.

Is there such a thing as a true religion?

For a few years of my life, I was firmly convinced that this existed, because everyone else must be wrong. Jehovah's Witnesses teach you that you are in the true religion. But I quickly learned that the other religions also claim this maxim for themselves. In advance, it was even possible to read in the newspaper that the Catholic sect has this claim, which has led to the fact that the Reformed sect and its members have been outraged.

The word religion comes from Latin and actually means worship. Worship is connected to faith. And – yes! – there is the true faith, but by no means a true religion. Faith is spirituality, which is characterized by spiritual beings believing in a God, liking to sing praises, pray, and share scriptures and insights. Faith also means wanting to work together for the good of our fellow human beings. Let's look at what the Bible says about faith.

WHAT DOES THE BIBLE SAY?

"Nevertheless, the hour is coming, and it is now, when believers will worship the Father with spirit and truth; for, indeed, the Father seeks such people. God is a spirit ..." (John 4:23–24)

God desires people who realize that God is Spirit, a spiritual being interested in truth. Man is created in the image of God – a spiritual being in a body that seeks to grasp the divinity in itself and the divine, i.e. God. Each and every one of us can and should say: I AM WHO I AM. For this realization, no religion is needed, but only faith in order to understand one's ego and the purpose of existence. Let's keep looking!

"Let us hold fast to the public declaration of our hope without wavering, for faithful is He who made the promise. And let us look out for one another to incite love and fine works, not giving up coming together ..." (Hebrews 10:23-25)

The faith should be proclaimed publicly and shared with other people. Likewise, other spiritual views should be listened to. People do this by coming together and exchanging ideas. In this gathering, conversations are meant to encourage each other to work out of love.

Where should this gathering take place? In a church, Kingdom Hall, hotel, or rented space?

Many denominations take this verse for themselves by declaring: "Only with us are you right!" So it happens that Catholics are among themselves, the Reformed are among themselves, the Jehovah's Witnesses are among themselves, the Adventists are among themselves, as well as all other religions in small or large groups. In this way, religions have a divisive effect. A spiritual being meets other people of a spiritual nature and enjoys the diversity of knowledge – one is not a Christian, a Jew, a Muslim, a Buddhist, a Catholic, a Reformed, etc., but only a spiritual being. If you leave the Catholic sect, you give up coming together from their point of view, even though you may now be in a different denomination. How do they come to tell you that you have given up on getting together?

As a spiritual being, coming together is important to you – for this reason, faith does not need religion. You can meet like-minded or not-so-like-minded people anytime, anywhere. By fewer like-minded people, I mean that as a spiritual being, you don't have to accept every opinion, but you can treat it respectfully. You don't care, because religion doesn't exist for you.

"The form of worship (religion)–or rather, faith–that is pure and unspotted from the standpoint of our God and Father is this: to look after orphans and widows in their tribulation, and to keep oneself from the world without spot." (James 1:27)

The true faith is characterized by the fact that it is for orphans and widows. is therefore characterised by solidarity. During the coronavirus crisis, children were separated from their elderly parents in nursing homes for a limited period of time. This should not be the case at all, and it is by no means permissible for the state to prescribe such a thing. It is painful for a spiritual being like you to have to go through this experience. You are not dependent on religion for solidarity. Faith alone is characterized by action. Faith is dead without these works. Faith offers comfort, fosters communication, is healing, protection, and love.

"But I wish all people were like myself. Yet, everyone has received their own gift from God." (1 Corinthians 7:7, 12)

A spiritual being has been given a gift by God, and sometimes he may have several talents. I'm Shogun (Peter Wehrli). My gift is protection, teaching is also a talent. The same goes for singing and writing – I do both with enthusiasm. In the 12th chapter of 1 Corinthians, some gifts are listed. They are: teaching, healing, speaking, singing. What is your gift? My gift, as I said, is protection. I protect lives and holy things. Again, God or the Divine gives the gift to YOU. And you inherited a lot from your parents of origin. It is not religion that determines who and what you are, but the Divine and yourself.

If you look at all religions, they are essentially characterized by these points:

- Belief
- Praying + Singing
- Meet
- Love/Encouragement
- Solidarity and support through various gifts If religions agree on this, why do they act in a divisive way?

Why do you think you have to choose whether you are a Christian or a Jew or a Muslim? A spiritual being has put into practice Jesus' words, "Come out of it, my people," by turning his back on religion. As long as you are within a religion, you will be considered a son/daughter of a harlot in the eyes of God.

Faith does not argue about other people's understanding of God, but grows by linking the old with the new, or by completely abandoning the old and willingly accepting the new.

Faith makes you realize that you are God, that you are a divine individual. This belief is lived outside of religion. And that's a good thing. Faith (not religion!) is what unites people. But this faith can only come about if you want to put the words of Jesus into practice in your life. Namely, "Get out of HER, my people."

It's time and important for you to stop being the son of a whore. If you stayed that way, you would go down with HER. How is this to be understood?

Look closely at the words of Revelation (chapters 17 and 18). We read that the wild beast turns against this harlot. "And the ten horns which thou sawest, and the wild beast, these shall hate the harlot, and shall devastate her, and make her naked, and shall devour her parts of flesh, and shall burn her utterly with fire. For God hath put it into their hearts to carry out his thoughts, giving their kingship to the wild beast, until the words of God shall be accomplished." (Revelation 17:16-18)

This description points to a tremendous change in religion. The political system would make religion naked. Nakedness in the biblical sense means to uncover truths, to point out the horrible deeds committed by religion: child abuse by clergy; financial gain through your own bank and financing of corrupt businesses; persecution and war, in which the faithful turn on each other like wild beasts; Wars of religion, where people of other faiths are killed by terror.

Orthodox churches have persecuted other Christian denominations in recent years, including Jehovah's Witnesses in Russia, sometimes with political support. In some Muslim countries, Christians and people of other faiths are also threatened or killed. Also with political support. In Switzerland, minarets and burqas were fought by political decisions. Politicians have already made decisions that crosses may no longer be hung in schools.

For some time now, it has been evident worldwide that politics is increasingly taking action against religion. Some people have even become godless people because of religion – atheism is on the rise. The sects (churches) are losing members.

Nevertheless, the harlot says, "I am by no means a widow, nor will I see sorrow." But if you take a close look at the worldview of religions, you will see that religion has no future. And those who cling too much to religion will perish because they no longer have a foothold. Such people have never learned what faith is all about.

"Get out of HER, my people!" Leave religion and live true spirituality, be a part of the big picture. Be connected to God, the source of all spiritual being! Look and see: The worldview of religion(s) is changing!

SO WHAT IS A CULT?

It is difficult, but NOT impossible, to work out a definition.

First of all, let's take a look at some definitions:

- a guru (a person or a kind of church council) who gathers others around him.
- a split from the major churches
- a political or religious party that teaches a different worldview than is generally known.
- a denomination that does not teach what the Bible teaches.

The latter definition not only assumes knowledge of the Bible, but also defines all other religions as sects because they deviate from the Bible. These include: Muslims, Jews, Far Eastern religions and others.

The first definition certainly makes it clear why I can call the Catholic Church, but also the Reformed Church, a sect.

Even "sect researchers" use the term religious special community so as not to be pejorative. This is because Christians are actually a Jewish sect, since Christianity originated from Judaism. After the Roman Empire recognized Christianity as the state religion, the Roman Catholic Church was born. The Reformation shook this sole position of omnipotence. The birth of the Reform Church was followed by others. From TODAY's point of view, they are all cults. How so? Let's come back to the question "What is a cult?". I would like to illustrate this with a simple picture – the Aquarium!

THE AQUARIUM

In an aquarium, the fish are among themselves, limited in their vision. You will never see the sea in most cases or even know what the sea is. It is the same with religion.

An aquarium is the habitat of ornamental fish. The fish are a select group in a prefabricated room that is set up to suit them.

This image is the best definition for religions and sects at the same time. These are groups of people who were born into a religion and thus into a religious community, or who have chosen it. But these people are never connected to the whole – that is, to the ocean, figuratively speaking. As a spiritual being, one can only experience true faith when one is connected to the Divine and the whole spiritual world. Every faith community is like such an aquarium: a group of people who often have human guidance and a different opinion than the other groups. Thus, it is a cult.

Definition of sect: A sect is when one accepts faith through a chosen or inborn religion (Latin: worship) or is brought up in it without being asked. (That definition is mine.)

Could this definition do justice to the word cult? Well, from my point of view, it is very appropriate, because faith is mixed with a religion that dictates what constitutes faith. So it is a cult because a worldview is prescribed. The spiritual being that one is does not need such a religion. "Get out of HER, my people" makes sense. And it's interesting that this request comes from Jesus himself – because he never wanted his ideas to become a religion with a dogmatic orientation. I should know – I am an adopted son of the Archangel Michael, who is Jesus. And I am of the people of the Pleiades[1]

I have looked with you at why the harlot of Babylon stands for religion. I have shown that it is important to give up religion. I have shown you that faith without religion is becoming more important than ever. You are a spiritual being who experiences growth as he swims in the ocean. Learn to question. Look over the horizon, get to know the magic of the spiritual world. You are extraordinary. No longer be the son of a whore. Get to know your true "mother". The Mother above – the heavenly Jerusalem. There you will find your parents of origin.

---

1 Pleiades, a star-studded people who have come to Earth. Short essay at the end of this work and through my story

THE JERUSALEM ABOVE – YOUR MOTHER

If you live your faith in conjunction with religion, you remain the son of a whore. But you have the opportunity, figuratively speaking, to get to know your spiritual mother. And your parents of origin. I understand if you're confused now. You have only now learned that religion is a prison. You were taught beliefs by your biological parents out of conviction. In addition, you learned a lot about customs and dogmas in religious education at school.

As well as what you are supposed to believe. And now I come along with my weird views. I am convinced that the truth will set you free and allow you to experience true spirituality. The Bible is one of many that can help YOU in your spirituality to understand things. Could it be that you have NEVER read the Bible? You wouldn't be the only one. Or have you read the Bible? Are you sure that you have already gained all the knowledge from this? Are you curious to grasp what the Jerusalem above is and why it is called Mother? I will accompany you a little along the way.

"The Jerusalem above, on the other hand, is free, and it is our mother."
(Galatians 4:26)

To understand these words, God, who is called the Father, helps us. The Jerusalem above is also referred to as a woman. In the Bible, symbolic symbolism is often used. In the 12th chapter of Revelation, we learn of a symbolic woman giving birth to a child. This also helps to understand what the mother is above. It is a spiritual being that can produce something. God is spirit, so the woman and mother is also spirit. Strictly speaking, it is the power – often described as the Holy Spirit.

For it is the Spirit who brings forth creation, as explained in the book of Genesis. In the 12th chapter of Revelation, the woman brings forth the Kingdom. Jerusalem became the capital of the kingdom of David and Solomon on earth – in Israel's heyday as a state. Jesus is described as a king, so the image of the heavenly Jerusalem is self-evident. It is a pure energy field of God, called Shekina in the Hebrew language. It is said that it is a female energy field. That's where I came from. More precisely, from the planet Alcyone, which is located near the constellation Taurus

So the mother above is the pure female energy field. I could certainly justify this in detail in biblical terms. But it is my intention that you yourself learn to broaden your spiritual horizons. But this might be helpful: there have always been gods and goddesses in the world of religion. It is from the energy field that your parents of origin come. There are several energy fields – I don't know how many. I, too, am always learning new things. In Norse mythology, there are nine worlds (this is referred to in the Marvel film "Thor"). This makes it clear that there must be more energy fields.

Some scholars often speak of twelve heavens or chakras. Most of you probably know that there are seven chakras. And at this time, humanity is in the process of ascending to the fifth dimension. Some are left behind in the third matrix.[2]

A woman is described in the biblical sense – as is the case with the harlot – as a symbol of religion. The Mother above is not just an energy field, but brings forth all that is necessary. The

---

2 dimension described in the Bible as a ladder to heaven. It stands for both parallel worlds and different stuffs that planet Earth and humans pass through. The first Matrix (the movie Matrix is a Contemporary document) was the Garden of Eden. It was not the fall of Adam and Eve, but an escape: Archaeological finds in the work of Michael Tellinger The slave race of the gods explains this. Spiritual people rise up, while religious people stay behind. (Jesus' parable in Matthew 24:40–41)

true faith of the past was also born out of it. After the destruction of the temple in 70 AD, it became clear that spirituality was no longer dependent on a house, temple or even religion. True faith is to be characterized by love. Faith without religion is true spirituality. Because, as has been shown, faith does not need religion.

So you have a choice: Do you want to live your faith with religion or without it? Do you want to have spiritual experiences by broadening your horizons? Choose the mother above instead of the harlot Babylon.

Reading and understanding the Bible or religious scriptures is one thing, but it is even more important to understand the divine. But I don't want to retranslate the Bible. Very well, the ancient scriptures can help you to understand your spiritual world. Because as spiritual beings, we on earth have always understood the spiritual through images and written testimonies. Before written products appeared, there was also a lot of oral transmission. So come with us on the journey of history to your being. Because that's how you experience your meaning in life, your life's purpose.

The old stories show you your spiritual past and lead you to the present, where the future is shaped. I'm going to look back, so to speak, covering Egypt, Assyria, Babylon, the Medes, Persia, Greece, and Rome. I will keep the most important points in mind. For more information, you will have to deal with historical sources and archaeological finds. My intention is to explain the spiritual world and not to write a historical treatise.

THE ANCIENT STORIES

The Creation

Jehovah (Yehjudah in the Hebrew language), some other Bible translations speak of God, created heaven and earth. The account of creation describes the origin of life on earth. Not the creation of the universe, although of course the universe was also created by God. The focus is on the planet Lady Sheyana, as the earth is called by us spiritual beings. In Greek mythology, she is rightly referred to as Gaia. In reference to this, the first woman was named Eve. Lady Sheyana, Gaia and Eve mean: mother of many people and lives. Thus, there is not only a heavenly mother from whom we come, but also an earthly mother.

The account of creation goes back in time to four billion years ago. If we were able to travel back in time, we would encounter a planet covered in water. The air would be enriched with carbon dioxide nitrogen. Land masses would have emerged from volcanic activity. The description is therefore scientifically correct.

As described, the earth's surface was desolate, empty and dark because diffuse light penetrated the atmosphere only gradually. And God said, "Let there be light," and there was light. The light sources, such as the sun, moon, stars, and the other galaxies, already existed in the Milky Way. In this solar system, life on Sheyana was not yet possible, but God's spirit hovered above the surface. Through the word, energy was used in a targeted way so that it could form. Even today, through our thoughts and words, we shape the reality in which we want to live. Therefore, the fourth day of creation seems confusing when it is declared that God created the sun and the moon and the stars. The creation account was written from the point of view of a human being. If man were on the surface of the earth, it would only now be visible to him what the light source would look like.

The atmosphere is also only now suitable for living on Sheyana. Now, through synthesis, green spaces – trees, forests – are created that break down the carbon dioxide.

And God said, "Let us make man in our image." The word "us" in the plural indicates that several Elohim (angelic beings) were involved, with the word Elohim in Hebrew standing for God, plural for gods. It is a fact: the Bible explains to the reader that God speaks to one or more creature(s). In the Bible, the firstborn Jesus is depicted as an instrument of co-creation, and the angels rejoiced when man was created (Book of Job and Proverbs). There are indications that the beings condensed their spiritual bodies, i. e. transformed them into material things, and thus became human beings. The other would mean that several beings were involved in the human project.

This leads to questions:

Were there more than one person now? If so, why was the focus only on two? Or were there just several beings involved in the human project?

The Bible declares: "And God proceeded to form man (man) out of the ground, and blew the breath of life into the body." In this way, man became a living soul. This statement would explain that several beings were involved in the human project, and created only this one human being. In other words, it would mean that many men existed after that. Whether one or more men, the woman did not yet exist. What is remarkable, however, is that the woman is a clone of the man. This is because the woman is formed by the bone marrow from the rib. And not necessarily in the same area as the man, because it says: "And the woman led God to the man." It is sexual attraction, a mental ability that we still have today by creating things or bringing them into life through attraction.

The history of the Pleiades shows that the people on planet Earth were settled by them. Some Ananuki then conducted experiments. So that man became a slave race in order to mine the gold. And the Garden of Eden was a kind of labor camp from which the first humans fled.

The woman is a clone of the man! There was a cloned woman of Adam: Eve. Lilith, his first wife, was created from the face of the earth like Adam, and therefore his equal. Eve means: Mother of all life! The Hebrew word woman means: female man! Cloning would basically only produce the same thing, but HERE the DNA was additionally altered with the energy in such a way that a counterpart was created! The clone is unique because a new creation has emerged! A slave race. Humans had 12 strands of DNA.[3]

---

3 Anunanki are a star people like the Pleiades, they are the Elohim (Michel Tellinger in The Slave Race of the Gods) is discussed. Archaeological finds refer to this people. It was known that it knew and knows the technology of cloning and genetic modification. (The procedure, the removal of Adam's rib, describes this accurately. The rib cage used to be open in humans. We have a scar tissue in the essential area where the rib was once removed. The DNA structure has been altered and the scars bear witness to the creation of Eve. Adam had two wives, Lilith and the clone Eve.

THE FALL OF MAN – A CONSCIOUS DECISION

It quickly becomes clear why the focus is on a couple when it is understood that just one decision can have far-reaching consequences for an entire territory or even the entire universe.

This is especially true if the decision made influences further developments. In the 5th chapter of Romans, it is explained that one person's misconduct had an effect on all people. (Romans 5:12)

Everything in the universe is subject to order (one could also say law, circumstances or love for it). There is even a High Council – a kind of conference between the Earth Alliance and other worlds. Job describes a conference between God and the angels. (Job 1 + 2)

The Galactic Federation is a council of several races, represented by their ambassadors.

This Council also adopts regulations, among other things. Man is a spiritual being with free will. After the Divine decided to educate human beings, a boundary was set out of love that human beings should not cross – the right to decide what would be good or unjust. "You must not eat of the tree in the middle of the garden, or you will die." All beings in the universe are immortal. So was man in Adam's time – Adam did not know death. What is dying? What is disease? What age? Because of our frail bodies, we are mortal. It can be damaged, for example if you climb a mountain and fall. Then our body dies. But death was never intended in the sense of the experiences that go hand in hand with growing old, getting sick and dying.

So we would only die if the legal boundaries associated with the body were exceeded. The tree and the fruit were a reminder and meant to show our limits. This was explained to the clone, the first wife Eve, because the memory that we are eternally living beings was taken away from her with the change in DNA. Eve was shrouded in the veil of oblivion. Thus, it was only a matter of time before curiosity took over to find out what dying was. You could also explain it like this: The mother tells her child not to touch the stove under any circumstances because he would burn his hand and suffer insane pain. A child who has never experienced this pain will still let it come down to it and exceed this set limit. This is exactly how we behaved at the beginning of humanity. Therefore, the woman ate of the forbidden fruit.

The angel who instigated it cleverly manipulated the woman through a lie.

This angel Yoah'Toh (among the Anunaki Enli) is known on earth as Lucifer. He resisted the Source by manipulating people through this action. He had once pledged to experiment with free will to find out what would happen if you broke away from the bond of love. It happened in the event that it went dark. His light and love were almost extinguished. Because he could no longer feel love, he became Satan. By eating the fruit, we have crossed a line. We wanted to know, "What is dying?" So we gave up eternal life. Eventually, it will be possible to live forever again, because it has been proven that we find enough evidence of eternal life in our DNA. Eventually, some of the Anunaki people with evil intentions altered the DNA in such a way that the dying was passed on to all humans. This is how death has come to all people.

LILITH AND ORAL GRATIFICATION

And God saw that it was not good for the man to be alone. He put the man into a deep sleep, took out a rib and shaped the woman. As already shown, cloning is described HERE. Eva was the first clone with altered DNA as a male counterpart. The first woman was Lilith, a goddess according to Sumerian scriptures. Lilith should be the man's equal. However, she rose up against the man by seeing herself as a goddess. The angels carried her to heaven for this reason. Lilith swore revenge by devouring Adam's descendants.

This has held up to this day, because the swallowing of the man's sperm is due to this revenge. The man had previously dated two women and had sex with both women. Now he was alone again with the clone Eva. She behaved submissively, but brought death by choosing to understand dying. She was mortal, Adam was still immortal. Rationally, he could have asked God to make a new, equally immortal clone. However, Adam decided to follow Eve out of emotion.

And so the fall of man is actually a development that has arisen out of love. Love also moves God to reverse this dying process. The first prophetic utterance was written down, thus explaining the plan of the Divine. The last prophetic utterance in the Bible book of Revelation also declares, "I will make all things new, and death will be no more." It is interesting to note that in the Bible book of Revelation we learn of the second death. This death no longer has anything to do with the first decision. And death would not pass on to all people again, no, the second death would only come into force for the person who would do something risky and thus end his life. Death was no longer for the collective.

The oral gratification (including swallowing) goes back to the story of Lilith, who swore revenge to devour Adam's descendants!

The age-old longing to sleep with two women, i.e. to perform sexual acts, goes back to references in the Bible and other scriptures that men had two wives and lived polygamy (Adam, Lamech, Abraham, Jacob). The book of Genesis 4:19 says, "And Lamech took two wives." The polygamous relationship and the threesome had taken hold.

EGYPT AND THE GODS

After the first murder committed by a brother, the murderer fled. Adam and Eve were born Seth. This son settled the Nile Delta. Man became a god, a legend. After the Flood, the descendants of Seth resettled in Egypt. There were great civilizations like Atlantis before the Flood, as well as cities on the Nile and elsewhere. After the Flood, people quickly had the idea of building cities again. Now, for the first time, we dive into the history of Egypt. Egypt became the center of a world power because it influenced history all the way to the Roman Empire.

The first reference in the scriptures to Egypt is already found in the birth of Seth. In Egyptian mythology (as can be read on Wikipedia, among others) there is no exact origin for the deity Seth. The Bible indicates that a son of Adam was so named. (Genesis 4:25) It also becomes clear that Seth and later his descendants settled in Egypt. Adam is referred to in the Bible as the Son of God. The idea of elevating oneself to a god was not alien. And indeed, Adam's son Seth allowed himself to be worshipped as a god by putting on the mask of a falcon.

Seth, the son of Adam, allowed himself to be worshipped as a god by putting on the mask of a falcon!

After the Flood, the Bible does not give us another glimpse of Egypt until Abraham goes there. Now Egypt appears to us as a military power with large metropolises. During the time when Moses grew up in the palace and later assumed his origins as a Hebrew, there was a rivalry between the one God, Jehovah, and the gods of Egypt. The exodus still plays an important role today. The 10 plagues were for 10 gods of Egypt. It was a powerful demonstration of the superiority of the one god over the several gods. But before that, we get an insight into an important event that teaches us spiritual beings to understand, what abilities we have and can develop, if we just want to. I'm talking about dream interpretation.

It happened that Jacob, through a ruse of his father-in-law, ended up in a polygamous marriage. Both women bore Jakob a total of 12 sons. One was Joseph. It was like this: Jacob loved Rachel more than Leah, and both women each brought a maid into the marriage. Jacob had the pleasure of sleeping with four women: Rachel, Leah, Silpah, and Bilhah. Jacob was rechristened in Israel as the progenitor of Israel and the 12 tribes. However, before the 12th son was born, it happened that 10 of the sons sold their youngest brother as slaves to Egypt. Joseph was an interpreter of dreams. Dream interpretation is one of the abilities that all spiritual beings carry within themselves as knowledge. But not all of them can implement them. You, too, have the opportunity and power to understand dreams, for they are messages that help you to master life in this duality. Most people seem to have forgotten this.

Egypt gave rise to the art of writing, dream interpretation, magic, astronomy, astrology and mathematics. There was a form of electrical energy, livestock, cultivation of wheat, many vegetables and temple complexes. Egypt was a military power and knew how to expand the country's borders through invasions. The Egyptians had the philosopher's stone at their disposal, because they were still able to use their energy in such a way that they could call things into their lives with pure energy – wealth and abundance and much more. Even the attraction was many times greater. Men gained power and prestige and women followed as much as a man wanted. The pyramids and magnificent buildings (from palaces and temples to libraries) were products of wealth and lasted well into the Roman Empire.

Another characteristic of us spiritual beings is magic. In the story of Moses and Pharaoh's priests, it becomes clear that we are able to transform energy into matter through magic. (Exodus 7:11) Although this magic is in us, it seems that magic is forbidden by God. Possibly to prevent abuse, because it is a powerful art that has also been used to manipulate people. Dark forces were able to take control of people. Magic should only be used for good purposes. So, as a spiritual being, you do indeed possess dream interpretation, magic, astrology, and astronomical knowledge. And the realization of space travel, because we, as spiritual beings, once came to the planet Sheyana, which is now known as Earth. The dark forces were able to put people into a deep sleep, so to speak, which they call control. The awakening, however, is now well advanced.

And you, as a reader, have begun to advance the awakening, otherwise you wouldn't be reading this book. The ancient stories teach us who we are, where we come from, and how to return to splendor, happiness, wealth, and abundance. Therefore, it may have been important for you to have this experience through religion for a long time before you became free. The old stories will always be a part of us, so that we don't make the same mistakes together again in the future. But the old stories should never again enslave us in a religion that only acts as a divisive.

You have incarnated in every epoch and thereby chosen to do what is done out of love. Namely, to direct the energy in such a way that life on earth was intended for: eternal life without religion and without further reincarnation. Or as it is written, "I will make all things new, and death will be no more, nor outcry and pain, for the former things have passed away." (Revelation 22)

You have been incarnated in every time period, and so you have not only experienced the Egyptian era, but every era. And each time, as a spiritual being, you have learned new things or had to deal with old things again until the lesson associated with this life was completed. In the year 2 B.C., Jesus was born in September. At the age of 30, he began to carry out his important task: redemption. He acted out of love so that Yoah'Toh could also be brought back to divine order. We have been experiencing this epoch since 1914 and since 2012 the awakening has been taking its full course. Since 2020, we have been in the final period in which religion is not only changing –, no! – but will disappear entirely.

It was Jesus Christ who said, "Get out of her, my people." Jesus also promised that He would return to finish what He had begun. You are a spiritual being who can see that religion is just a prison. The old stories are a help so that you can see where you come from, what you are and where you will go. Because you are now living in the here and now, in the present, to shape your future. Don't look to the past to judge yourself any longer. Everything was done out of love. And selfless love can be lived by unlocking the full potential of your being. Be absorbed in the fact that you are learning to walk on water, to do things that become possible through your mind, your energy. Create your reality!

Be no longer the son of a harlot, but be free like our mother above (the Jerusalem above).

MY STORY IS ALSO YOURS

Four billion years ago, I came to the planet Lady Sheyana, better known to you as Gaja Earth, with 23 other light beings. What happened after we had condensed our light bodies with dust, you have already learned under the old stories. After the dark lord Lucifer manipulated humans, his seed sprang into the descendants of Cain's bloodline with the goal of enslaving humans. Another bloodline would grind the serpent's head. Until that would happen, I was left behind as an observer with the order to cut down the tree of life. I have already revealed to you something about your spiritual mother. It was this mother who ensured that Abel's bloodline would continue to produce seeds, i. e. children. Jesus is the only being of light incarnated directly in the womb.

Many other "demigods" have often been born by procreation. For angels saw the women on the earth and kindled lust, and so they took human form and the women, which caused the earth to be strewn with evil deeds. During the flood, the island of Atlantis also sank – yes! – they really existed. What you have learned in school has been written under the manipulation of the dark power. Some of the history actually needs to be rewritten. But that's not my job. But the Deep State began at that time. The Egyptians were annihilated. Nevertheless, you survived. Today, in the 21st century, Bill Gates emerged from this bloodline. In 2020, he gave the order to reduce humanity.

I was incarnated in 1973 so that I could help with the many other light beings (there is an alliance of eight other planets and entities with the planet Lady Sheyana) to advance the healing and transformation into the 5th dimension. The experiment is then aborted and Lucifer is tied to the Light and Source of Love to lead people into the Golden Age. I'd like to share my story with you a little bit after I've already covered the finale.

Come back to the 6th century BC to the time when King Hezekiah reigned. There I was Shemyahiah, a temple guard in the temple that King Solomon had built. The Assyrian army conquered one city after another. When Lachish fell, the conquest of Jerusalem was to be expected at any time, for the serpent's descendants would do anything to wipe out the bloodline of Abel. The mother above would then cease to exist. But the Divine did not stand idly by, it sent the Archangel Michael, who killed 185,000 Assyrian soldiers to save the bloodline of Abel.

I spent another life as Simon, who was given the name Peter by Jesus. Before I was called by Jesus, I spent time as a fisherman and belonged to the fishermen's guild. I was able to live well on my income. I found the Jews who collected the taxes to be bloodthirsty, which is why I despised them. I knew a lot about the tax system. This was also the reason why Rabbi Yeshuaah (the son of Joseph of Nazareth) asked me if the kings were tax-free. I answered in the affirmative.

I am always spontaneous, aggressive, helpful, determined, merciful, reckless, courageous and also a little naïve. Love overflows in me, which, by the way, is my greatest quality – yes! – love. I shine brighter than the morning star when my time comes to follow my vocation and fulfill my mission with passion.

Even today, I live tax-free through the knowledge of how the system works or I would only have to pay just 30 francs in tax annually and that since 2019. I think I can rightly say that I am a descendant of the Pleiades and a descendant of the house of David. I had already shown in my earlier incarnation as Simon Peter that I did not support the system at all. How I achieved this is another story. However, I take to heart the words of Jesus:

and to the question: What is truth? I answer like Jesus:

I am the truth, I am the way, I am the life

In every life I have excelled. If I have ever radiated anything negative, God protect my fellow human beings. You never want to experience my dark side. My energy is destructive. I am rather inconspicuous, appear in your life at short notice and disappear as I came. As if it were yesterday, which is true, I was moved when I saw Yeshuah (Joseph) walking on the Sea of Galilee.

I spontaneously got out of the boat and only sank when I was distracted, lost eye contact and doubts arose in me. Just as I can remember past lives, so could you. But if you don't succeed, don't worry. Live in the here and now! But you can be sure that you have helped me in one way or another and that we have met over the past few years.

What is it like for you to know what you have experienced? How do you look at rebirth? What questions do you have? It is not my intention to answer all your questions. Rather, you should form your own opinion and go in search of the right answers.

How do you unfold your potential in spirituality?

Meditation is the best way to make progress in spirituality. You will: discover telepathic abilities; learn to understand manipulation and use it usefully; learn lucid dreaming; get to know astral travel; even learn how to create your own reality. You will also be introduced to magic and energy work and learn how to use tarot cards usefully. In the end, you will be empowered to bring forth wealth and abundance. You're going to become; which is expressed in the most powerful words: I AM WHO I AM! You will travel to the past and the future. Experience what it means to be invisible. You will learn dream interpretation, self-healing and other healing methods (herbalism). In this way, you will live a life that allows you to stay healthy.

WHAT IS MEDITATION?

Meditation is a workout for your body and mind. Especially for your mind, to be able to bring out your potential from the subconscious and your intuition. You program your brain, create new synapses (new connections) to eventually even manifest things that you consciously want in your life.

Meditation refers to traditions that have been handed down for thousands of years. Since the 20th century, they have increasingly been practiced and researched in a secular manner in the Western world. An essential element of meditative techniques is the conscious control of attention. Depending on the context of the practice, the practice of meditation is intended to bring about lasting positive changes in thinking, feeling and experiencing. Or lead to specific religiously defined insights and states. Effects of meditation training on cognition, affect, brain function, immune system and epigenetics, as well as on mental health, have been scientifically proven, some of them to a high standard.

Meditation means being intimately connected to the Divine and to oneself. Do you know the story "Aladdin and the Magic Lamp"? Aladdin finds a lamp in a cave. When he rubs against it, a spirit (known as a djinn) is released. In some stories it is explained that he can only grant three wishes, which is not true. You know, the Spirit says every time, **"Your wish is my command!"** This spirit is God, the Divine, among the indigenous people it is the great spirit Manitu, elsewhere Jehovah, simply God, Alljah. When you meditate and focus and visually shape your life, you express what you want through your thoughts and desires, and God, i. e. the Spirit, then says:
"Your wish is my command!" It was not in vain that Jesus said, "Ask, and it shall be given to you by the Father." The

important thing is that you don't worry or have any doubts. Not only does faith symbolically move mountains, but you could build an energy field that can even literally move mountains.

There are different forms of meditation.

Zen meditation is a non-objective form of meditation that is about nothing less than the realization of our true being. In the language of Zen, this means realizing Buddha-nature. Other terms include: self-knowledge; realize the Dao; realize the wisdom of the heart with the clear-sightedness of the spirit; experience our divine nature; to experience the truth or reality.

The most well-known exercise is zazen, sitting in contemplation. The upper body is erect, the shoulders are slightly backwards and pulled down (bear shoulders) so that the chest opens. The hands are in your lap. The eyes are only slightly open and look about a meter forward at the floor. But the gaze is not focused outwards, but goes inwards. The head, the neck as well as the entire upper body are kept upright. The lordosis (prevention) of the lumbar spine is preserved, so do not pull up the pelvis in front!

Which sitting postures are beneficial and which are not?

Probably the most well-known meditation posture is the full lotus position. Both legs are crossed over each other, the soles of the feet look upwards. This posture requires a lot of flexibility. Modified forms are: the half lotus seat and the quarter lotus seat. A more comfortable variant for many people is the knee seat (also called diamond seat), either on a higher cushion or a stable meditation bench.

Another popular sitting variant is the Burmese sitting posture, in which the legs are no longer crossed together as in the lotus positions, but simply lie loosely in front of each other directly on the mat.

And then there is the option of meditating on a chair. The most important thing in zazen is to choose a sitting posture in which you can sit and meditate for a longer period of time (10-30 minutes) without pain.

Under no circumstances should one torture oneself for the sake of optics and ambition. That would have been a loss of purpose!

I start in the morning with the Kneipp technique, the predominantly cold rinsing. There is also the alternating method (alternating cold and hot). Afterwards I sit naked on a cushion on a chair in all weathers – with both feet connected to the earth. All this on the balcony or terrace. Sometimes I treat myself to masturbation at the end. I also like to drink warm water every day. Sitting lightly on the outer edge of the chair, it is best. With or without affirmations.

There are also guided meditations that are very good to listen to. And good video tutorials.

Great attention is paid to breathing in all spiritual teachings. It is a link between body and mind. Through our breathing, we can both relax the body and calm the mind. Our normal everyday breathing is often too shallow and much too short. Breathing says a lot about us: Are we short of breath? Are we out of breath? Have we run out of breath? Are we breathless? Etc.

Zen breathing is not a special kind of breathing. It's more our natural breathing, which we usually don't practice anymore. Therefore, it is necessary to first become aware of the correct breathing. For Zen meditation, you have to deepen your breathing and breathe more slowly. Breathing is only done through the nose, the mouth is closed. The exhalation is longer than the inhalation. At the end of the exhalation, one should linger in the hara (lower abdomen). During the exhale, try to bring the consciousness down (where the hands are in the lap during meditation), and make sure that the consciousness remains down there during the inhale. Practice calm, silent breaths.

I myself often use deep breaths in my stomach and down into my pelvis. These breathing exercises are more intense than the silent ones. With breathing, we can open the entire Kundalini[4] and all the chakras. I breathe in through my nose and out through my mouth. There is also the Wim Hof technique.[5] Try holding your breath for a few minutes as well.

I would like to tell you an anecdote from my life. I was happily married to Franziska for 12 years. One day she showed me a bill. She was horrified and exclaimed: "How are WE supposed to pay this bill of 8000 francs?" I said, "Don't worry! God cares for us." I looked at the bill and made my request to God through meditation. We were paid 8000 francs by the insurance company because we were entitled to this sum as a surplus. "Here," I said, "are the 8,000 francs."

---

4 Kundalini (Sanskrit, feminine, कुण्डलिनी, kuṇḍalinī śakti, a form of devi, kundalini snake, "serpent power") refers to an etheric force in humans described in tantric scriptures. In Tantrism, one speaks metaphorically of a sleeping, coiled snake (Sanskrit: kundala "coiled, coiled"), as it lies in every human being at the lower end of the spine, in the lowest chakra. Wikipedia

5 The Wim Hof technique is a meditation technique developed by Wim Hof. Explanations can be found in his books. The extreme sportsman is also known as the Iceman. A similar therapy technique is the Kneipp technique.

Franziska was not only skeptical about my statement, but also enraged: "You with your God Jehovah!" I have proved that the Spirit says, "Your desire is my command."

Learn meditation, mindfulness, focusing, and visualizing. With prayer, you have a powerful tool to create the reality you want with words. You strengthen your immune system because you reprogram your consciousness towards health. Positive thoughts set by suggestion encourage you to reduce, or even eliminate, anger, rage, stress, and blasphemies that are responsible for high blood pressure, cancer, and dementia.

Get a lot of information about health as soon as you can – my book, but also other works and magazines – because your subconscious, as you deal with health, immediately takes action and works for you. In this way, it automatically finds the solution to your request.

Meditation can do something very special: make lucid dreaming possible!

WHAT IS LUCID DREAMING?

Lucid dreaming is awesome! Lucid dreaming is a dream in which you, as the dreamer, create your dream world. You want to be Supergirl and be able to fly? Fly to all the places you want to visit!

Science speaks of a lucid dream. A **lucid dream**, from the Latin lux, lucis "light", is a dream in which the dreamer is aware that he is dreaming. Paul Tholey, psychologist and the most important German lucid dream researcher, put it this way: **"Lucid dreams are those dreams in which one has complete clarity about the fact that one is dreaming and can act according to one's own decision."** 6

For this definition, Tholey drew on the philosopher Celia Green and the psychologist Charles Tart.

Tholey and the American psychologist Stephen LaBerge are the two central pioneers in the field of modern lucid dream research. Everyone probably has the ability to experience lucid dreams, and one can learn to induce this form of dreaming. There are various techniques for this. A person who can purposefully experience lucid dreams is also called Oneironaut (from Gr. oneiros "dream" and nautēs "sailor"). The technique is to put oneself into a trance state or waking dreaming through meditation and suggestive thinking. Lucid dreaming is not an astral journey or daydreaming, although it is similar. You also dream with your eyes open (not necessarily).

---

6 The quote can be found in Wikipedia – lucid dream. Paul Tholey, German psychologist and dream researcher, is also a pioneer in lutid dreaming in his journal (Die Zeitschrift Bewusst, which he himself founded in 1989).

But, as explained, you can shape your dreams or experience something intensely while dreaming. For example, I once dreamed how all the glass in my apartment was shattered by an explosion. I walked over it naked and injured my right foot in a dream. When I woke up, everything in my apartment was fine, but my right foot hurt.

Lucid dreaming, if you are inexperienced in spirituality, is the premier class, as I affectionately call it. Astral travel and telepathic abilities are also to be found in this premier class. Everyone learns in spirituality to grow at their own pace. I suddenly discovered that I can make myself invisible. I realized that I can do it, but I haven't really been able to fathom HOW I do it, only WHAT I do. It's about moving at a different frequency than your environment. But for me, I tend to do it spontaneously, without understanding the HOW. But it would be great to get to the bottom of the HOW and be able to retrieve it at any time. Now the subconscious helps me. Real magic (not just a cheap magic show) is possible. Self-healing helps you stay healthy forever.
(In my book "Never Again Sick – Stay Healthy Forever & the Lies of the Pharmaceutical Industry" I show you how to achieve this goal of staying healthy forever.)

It's worth reading my works. They complement each other and always let you discover something new.

So, if you choose the right mother and the whore of Babylon leaves, worlds will open up to you that are magnificent. You get to know your true origins, who you are and where you come from. This may also be scary. Then learn to face the fear. Because fear is a bad advisor. You are kept small by fear. Religions have ruled people through fear. And I think the Bible is a book that contains a lot of wisdom. But it also fosters fear by telling of the punishing God, which is a contradiction to the love of God taught through Christ. Nevertheless, the Greek scriptures and gospels are associated with a punishing God. Over time, I was able to understand that the Ten Commandments are commands that encourage people to do exactly what is not actually desired in any way. Because man is a spiritual being who never understands words like NOT.

As an example: **"Thou shalt NOT kill."** But the Spirit understands, **"Thou shalt kill."** The use of "thou shalt" is a reference to a command. "Thou shalt love thy neighbor as thyself" is also **a command**. Do you notice the difference? The word NOT is not used under any circumstances.

The original 10 commandments were different anyway. I was able to connect with the Akashic Records (some call it the Morphic Field, [7] maybe you know another term) and experience the real 10 Commandments.

1st Commandment: You are the only God. There are no other gods above you to harm you. You are eternally connected to Source.

2nd Commandment: Your name is holy. You are unique. You are "I AM". It is through consciousness that you define yourself. You are all and one.

3rd Commandment: You are the Truth, the Way, and the Light. Do not harm other beings or yourself. Be mindful of creation.

4th Commandment: Thou shalt neither kill nor lie. Thou shalt love thy neighbor as thyself.

---

7 Morphic field: and Asharka chronicles are meant to be one and the same, comparable to a large library of knowledge that every human being can retrieve. It is often described as a hypotetic field, the British biologist Rubert Sheldrake has made the discovery. (In movies like Star Wars, it's described as an all-encompassing force. In the Bible, it's the Spirit.)

5th Commandment: Honor and respect every living being and never withhold what is good. Honor your father and mother.

6th Commandment: Desire to experience all riches and abundance, and share this with men and animals, for abundance and riches are your right. Thou shalt desire all things, promote all living beings, and never withhold from them.

7th Commandment: Be fruitful and grow. You should use your skills for the good of all. Thou shalt reproduce.

8th Commandment: Thou shalt empower thyself. Thy will shall be done – as it is in heaven, so also on earth.

9th Commandment: Thou shalt never steal.

10th Commandment: Love many women and give life. Thou shalt choose life. Create your reality that makes it worth living in.

You may have had a similar experience when questioning this field. Give it a try! If you learn other words, write them down. It was very exciting for me to experience these words in this way, and these commandments are much more beautiful, more loving and do not keep us small or in fear in any way. Because the Ten Commandments in the Bible cause us to be afraid that if we obey the commandments correctly, we will be punished or commit a sin.

Because mistakes or "sins" are a motivation to learn to improve. Sins can also mean missing a target. In archery, if we miss the target or overshoot it, we learn through good technique to use the bow in such a way that we hit the target.

That's why affirmations and suggestions begin with "I AM." For the words I AM are very powerful. This is how we enable humans to create anything.

For example, a commandment can simply be started with "I AM" instead of the command formula "Thou shalt".

I AM the only God, and above me I have no other gods to harm me.

I AM: This is my name and it is sacred to me.

I AM Love and therefore I love everything and everyone.

I AM the Truth, the Life and the Way.

I AM connected to all and I am one with all.

I AM honest in everything.

I AM Peace.

I AM ready to grow and give life.

I like to be with other beings.

I like to be united through sex.

In general, affirmations that begin with "I AM" are more powerful and bring forth a powerful reality. Jesus' statement "I am the way, the truth and the life" has been misunderstood by Christians of all denominations. The point is that every human being may attain Christ's consciousness, nay, rather must attain it. It is by no means true that one comes to God only through Christ. This is a narrow-minded thought. It is only through the Christ-consciousness that one becomes the God or the divine individual that man has always been. By forgetting and consciously keeping the senses small and by changing our DNA, we have fallen into a slave existence.

Until mid-1995, our DNA consisted of a total of 12 strands, 2 strands of which also exist in dense physical matter. In 1996, in preparation for the ascension energies, the 13th strand was formed.

So the 2 strands of DNA that have been discovered by science so far reach into the physical world visible to all.

Another 10 strands of DNA are located on the etheric and upper vibrational realms of the astral plane. These 10 strands of DNA have increasingly deactivated or limited their function during the descent into the depths of duality and dense matter. The reason for this was the decreasing connection of human beings to their own "Supreme Source", their own divine self and soul.

During the 288,000-year cyclical descent period, especially in the last cycle, there was mainly manipulation of the physical 2-stranded DNA (predominantly from the Anunakis and, to a lesser extent, the other 10 strands of DNA).

The 13th strand of DNA became necessary to prepare the ascension process of humanity. The 13th strand runs through the other 12 and ensures the possibility of connection with a person's own "Supreme Origin". It is only through this that the construction and activation of the light body has become possible.

The 12-stranded DNA and also the 13-stranded DNA (which do not have a double helix shape) are primarily transmitting and receiving stations of information stored at higher levels and the corresponding exchange of information.

By beginning to seek my Heavenly Father as a child, I began to connect with the Divine. At the age of twelve, I had an understanding of the Bible and theological knowledge that astonished most theologians around me. So, unconsciously, I started to build up the 12 DNA strands without ever knowing anything about them before 2023. Since 2018 I understand that my name is Shogun Peter from Wehrli. From 2017 to 2023, I made greater spiritual developments than in previous years.

I discovered my telepathic abilities in 2020. I was also able to realize that I can make myself invisible. I learned Tarot and Vedic Astrology. In addition, I discovered my psychic abilities, magic and herbal medicine. Since 2008 I have been empowered to practice self-healing. Through acting, I've made a connection to my inner child. I learned to remember where I came from and who I am. My name Shogun alone means "the divine dragon" or "dragon god", Peter means "the rock" and Wehrli means "guardian of the army" or "keeper of holy things".

However, I am at the very beginning of my knowledge and still have a long way to go to develop my skills. Since I left organized religion, I have grown tremendously spiritually.

Abandoning and dissolving religion leads to truth, and that truth leads to freedom. Freedom begins with the realization that you are never the thinker. The moment you begin to observe the thinker, a higher level of consciousness is activated. You realize that there is an infinitely large realm of intelligence beyond thought, of which thinking is only a tiny fraction. You begin to awaken.

Awakening means never having finished learning. In the same way, awakening means being allowed to see and understand things that are within you. It's overflowing. Jesus' words really make sense when he said, "I am the water of eternal life." When I began to understand the Bible, it became my intention that everyone should know this. That hasn't changed in any way. Today I would like to share my new knowledge with you.

The religions, i. e. the harlot Babylon (the Great), brought bloodshed. Dissidents and vegans were persecuted. Herbal medicine was almost wiped out by the witch burnings. Self-healing and various energies have been erased from people's memories.

It took me a long time to understand what Jesus' call meant. Today I would like to share this knowledge both with people who have recognized this, but even more so with people who are still trapped in religions.

The new knowledge is spreading and I would like to help bring this knowledge to the people. I hope to have broadened your horizons with this work.

Your Shogun

WORDS AND EXPLANATIONS (GLOSSARY)

Lady Sheyana : Is Goddess Gaja a word from my light language of the Pleiades also found in the language of some Native Americans. Planet Earth is female.

Pleiades: A star people and at the same time a constellation Pleiads are a star cluster near the zodiac sign Taurus Aldebaran is a fixed star (destroyed by the Death Star in the Star Wars saga) of course Aldebaran is still visible in the starry sky like the Pleiades.

With Anunaki and the Atlanteans, Aryans, the Pleiades also belong to star peoples and the people called them Elohim – gods. The Pleiades have original blue skin colors, as shown in the movie Avatar and in the children's series The Smurfs. The Tartars and Aryans are the sons of Japheth of the descendant of Noha. The Slavs and other European peoples emerged from it. Pleiades are often wise people with blond hair with blue eyes or some like me brown hair and brown eyes.

Michel Tellinger describes in detail in his work: **"The Slave Race of the Gods – The Secret History of the Anunaki and their Mission on Earth"** because he refers to archaeological finds and the many stone tablets that in turn describe the history of Edin. If you are willing to do research, you will realize that the story has been falsified, whether consciously or unconsciously, at least nothing was ever learned about the Tartars and Pleiades in school. In Japanese culture, my people are called Subaru, it is a fact that every person who sees a Subaru on the street also sees a reference to our people. The time, epoch begins, when more and more people will hear from us.

Kundalini: Is Sanskrit means coiled snake It is laid along the spine and connects the chakers. In the children's series – Dragon Ball, the chakras are symbolically represented as spheres that can evoke the dragon Jenglong. And then the dragon fulfills a wish.

In our case, it is the seven chakras and through the rise of the Kundalini serpent we are able to manifest and fulfill our desires.

All the stories in movies and books and the stone tablets contain the knowledge that man is a Divine Being who is much more powerful than he is aware of. In the film – the fifth element, there is a hint that man originally possessed 12 strands of DNA. This knowledge is scientifically proven in biology, phylosophy.

Dimension: There are parallel worlds and several earths at the same time and everything in the here and now, the Bible describes it figuratively as a ladder to heaven. Our planet is ascending and that is why we are seeing the big changes so quickly on the outside. In the Spiritual World, we also speak of Portal Days. These portals are used by people to travel to other worlds.

Matrix: Holographic view of the world, everything consists only of vibrations. The words of Morpheus: "The Matrix surrounds you when you look out the window, or go to church, or to work, the Matrix is omnipresent." It is, so to speak, our playing field so that we can experience matter. Paul himself explains in 2 Corinthians chapter twelve verses 2-4 that he speaks of the third heaven. The 3rd matrix is today's world, which is in the process of ascending into the 5th dimension. The first was Edin.

Rate
this **book**
on our
website!

www.novum-publishing.co.uk

FÜR AUTOREN A HEART FOR AUTHORS À L'ÉCOUTE DES AUTEURS MIA KAPΔIA ΓIA ΣYΓΓΡ
FÖR FÖRFATTARE UN CORAZÓN POR LOS AUTORES YAZARLARIMIZA GÖNÜL VERELIM SZÍ
PER AUTORI ET HJERTE FOR FORFATTERE EEN HART VOOR SCHRIJVERS TEMOS OS AUTC
 INKÉRT SERCE DLA AUTORÓW EIN HERZ FÜR AUTOREN A HEART FOR AUTHORS À L'ÉCOU
АÇÃO ВСЕЙ ДУШОЙ К АВТОРАМ ETT HJÄRTA FÖR FÖRFATTARE Á LA ESCUCHA DE LOS AUTOI
MIA KAPΔIA ΓIA ΣYΓΓΡΑΦΕΙΣ UN CUORE PER AUTORI ET HJERTE FOR FORFATTERE EEN I
ZÖINKÉRT SERCE DLA AUTORÓW EIN HERZ FÜF
АÇÃO ВСЕЙ ДУШОЙ К АВТОРАМ ETT HJÄRTA FÖI

The author

Shogun Drachengott, also known as Shogun Peter
from the House of Wehrli, was born in Switzerland
in 1973. After attending secondary and vocational
school, he worked in various areas: as a gardener,
kitchen worker, theologian, actor and philosopher.
In his free time, the author likes to devote himself to chess, cycling, swimming, reading and, of
course, writing. Over the past few years, he has
been extensively involved in herbal medicine and
magic. He impressively demonstrates his theological knowledge and philosophical reflection, which
he applies every day in his practice as a spiritual
coach, in his first work "You are the son of a
whore". The author's declared goal is to support
his readership in gaining new insights. He does not
prescribe ready-made answers, but motivates you
to find them yourself.

The publisher

> *He who stops getting better stops being good.*

This is the motto of novum publishing, and our focus is on finding new manuscripts, publishing them and offering long-term support to the authors.
Our publishing house was founded in 1997, and since then it has become THE expert for new authors and has won numerous awards.

Our editorial team will peruse each manuscript within a few weeks free of charge and without obligation.

You will find more information about novum publishing and our books on the internet:

w w w . n o v u m - p u b l i s h i n g . c o . u k